The GIRL with BIG, BIG QUESTIONS

by
BRITNEY WINN LEE

illustrated by
JACOB SOUVA

beaming ☀ books
MINNEAPOLIS

There once was a girl with twinkling eyes

and a very curious mind.

This girl was always asking questions

whose answers weren't easy to find.

The world is so very interesting!

She wanted to learn all she could,

from what makes a plane stay in the sky

to what makes each person good.

Her days were filled with adventures galore,

since her mind was so full of wonder.

How long can a turtle stay in its shell?

Why does lightning come before thunder?

Why can't people live on the moon?

What happens to stars when they fall?

When will you let me stay up all night?

Why even have bedtime at all?

What does the dog do while I'm at school?

Hey, how was the whole world made?

And why do we have big hearts that can feel

hurt and upset and afraid?

Could I fly if I got a good running start?

The nearest volcano is . . . where?

Are monsters real? What's Spanish for *blue*?

Is it okay to cut my own hair?

From the moment she opened her eyes for the day

to the time she was tucked into bed,

she'd ask and ask and ask and ask

every question that popped in her head.

At first her neighbors, teachers, and friends tried to answer her wonder-filled mind. But after a while, their encouraging smiles were replaced by the rolling of eyes.

She noticed her questions were making them tense,

and one day her class hit their limit.

After she asked a dozen things about clouds,

the class hollered, "Please stop! Just quit it!"

Embarrassed, the girl tried to quiet her thoughts

and not raise a voice so curious

so that no one would be too uncomfortable

or even worse, furious.

But one day, she found the nest of a bird

built low and exposed near the ground.

Why would a nest not be in a tree?

she wondered and then looked around.

She was all by herself with no one to ask,

so she ran to the library shelves.

She read about cities and the lack of safe places

for birds to build nests for themselves.

Like hunting for treasure, she

searched and learned

more answers that

made her frown.

With an urgent report, she announced to her class:

The class, now moved by this information,

asked questions about how to embark

on a project to help both the birds and their neighbors

by planting more trees in their parks.

The girl knew then that big questions are good

and answers aren't just things to know.

They are things to discover alongside each other.

Asking questions is how we all grow!

This one's for Jason, whose mind
has always been magic to me.

—B.W.L.

For Dennis, the patient and loving
recipient of many, many questions.

—J.S.

Text copyright ©2021 Britney Winn Lee
Illustrations copyright ©2021 Beaming Books

Published in 2021 by Beaming Books, an imprint of 1517 Media.
All rights reserved. No part of this book may be reproduced without the written permission of the publisher.
Email copyright@1517.media. Printed in the United States of America.

27 26 25 24 23 22 21   1 2 3 4 5 6 7 8

Hardcover ISBN: 978-1-5064-7378-9
Ebook ISBN: 978-1-5064-7406-9
Library of Congress Cataloging-in-Publication Data

Names: Lee, Britney Winn, author. | Souva, Jacob, illustrator.
Title: The girl with big, big questions / by Britney Winn Lee ; illustrated
by Jacob Souva.
Description: Minneapolis : Beaming Books, 2021. | Series: The big, big
series ; 2 | Audience: Ages 5-8. | Summary: "In a world that doesn't
always welcome big questions, a persistent and inquisitive girl keeps
asking them anyway--because asking questions is how we learn and grow"--
Provided by publisher.
Identifiers: LCCN 2020056503 (print) | LCCN 2020056504 (ebook) | ISBN
9781506473789 (hardcover) | ISBN 9781506474069 (ebook)
Subjects: CYAC: Stories in rhyme. | Questions and answers--Fiction.
Classification: LCC PZ8.3.L49918 Gir 2021 (print) | LCC PZ8.3.L49918
(ebook) | DDC [E]--dc23
LC record available at https://lccn.loc.gov/2020056503
LC ebook record available at https://lccn.loc.gov/2020056504

VN004589; 9781506473789; MAY2021

Beaming Books
510 Marquette Avenue
Minneapolis, MN 55402
Beamingbooks.com

BRITNEY WINN LEE is an author, editor, and non-profit director living in Shreveport, Louisiana, with her creative husband and big-hearted son. She serves as the full-time director of Noel Community Arts Program and the part-time editor and content coordinator for Red Letter Christians. With a BA in religious studies and a master's degree in nonprofit administration, Britney has worked for over a decade in faith- and justice-based creative community-building.

JACOB SOUVA is an illustrator who lives in Upstate New York with his wife and two boys. He's passionate about equipping kids with language to navigate their emotional well-being, laugh at silly things, and be inspired by big stories. Jacob works digitally and loves to experiment with texture and color.